Sage and Cedar

Messages from the other place

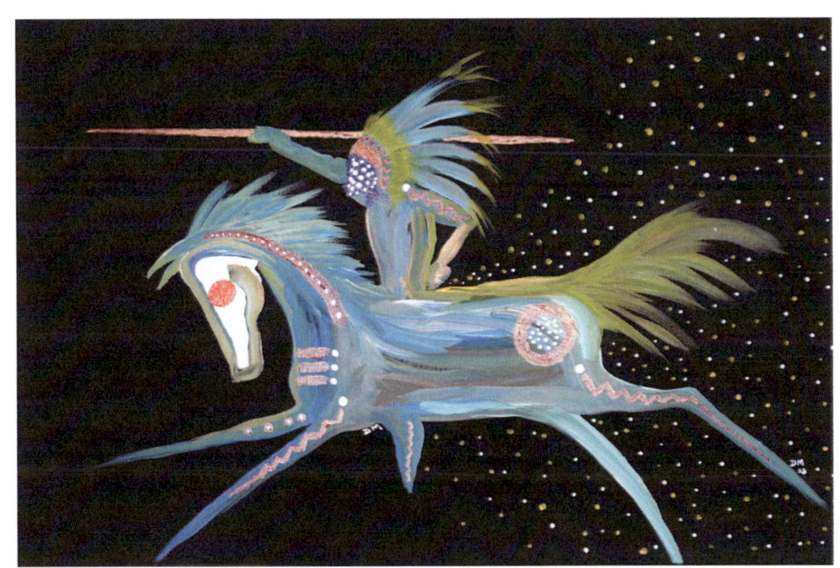

Stories and artwork
by Darrell Marcus Kills In Sight

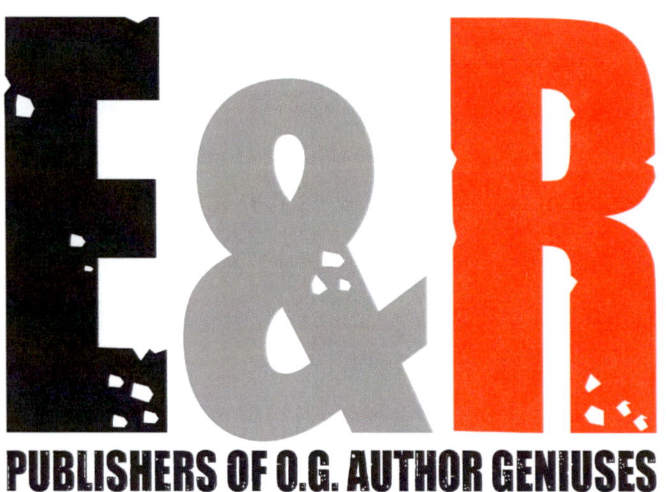

Published by E&R Publishers
New York, NY, USA
An imprint of MillsiCo Publishing, USA
www.EandR.pub

Your guarantee of quality
As publishers, we strive to produce every book to the highest commercial standards. The printing and binding have been planned to ensure a sturdy, attractive publication that should provide years of enjoyment. If your copy fails to meet our high standards, please inform us, and we will gladly replace it.
admin@millsi.co

ISBN: 9798990521704 Hardcover
ISBN: 9798990521711 Softcover
ISBN: 9798990521728 Ebook
Library of Congress Control Number: On file
First Edition

Dedication.

This book I have written for my people—to tell the stories of spirit and propertity.

This art is from my soul. It flows through me from the other place. I leave it for my people. The children. To take our past into their future.

Darrell Marcus Kills In Sight

Rainbow Woman

As the warrior was coming into his homeland, it started to rain. It was raining heavily so he waited under trees with his horse. It rained so hard that the water was now flowing by. The rain brought the breeze of the northern wind. The rain stopped and the warrior got on his horse to face the golden sunlight and beautiful rainbow—then a second rainbow but in this rainbow he could see something at the end of one of the hills. The warrior rode his horse in that direction, and as he came to the hill he saw a woman standing there in a dressed hide. It had porcupine quill the same colors as the rainbows.

When her long black hair drifted in the wind, he could the see rainbow colors there too. As he got close to her she turned towards the storm clouds and sang a song. She burned sage and cedar with the smell of rain as he drifted into a dream of the woman in colors.
When he came to, she was sitting by him and she offered him water and berries. She gave her story of the rain and that it represented her people. The rainbows were his mother and father, and the storm was her grandparents, that bring the rain to earth.

He told her how he would like to be with her but he had the sense she was leaving again. He told her he was alone in his life. The woman smiled and said she was glad he could come for she has been seeking a heart from the soul of the earth. Her strength was fading and she sought a man to be her soul in strength. She said the other rainbow behind her needed strength, so the two rainbows began with a love of rain and earth to grow her children, the rain.

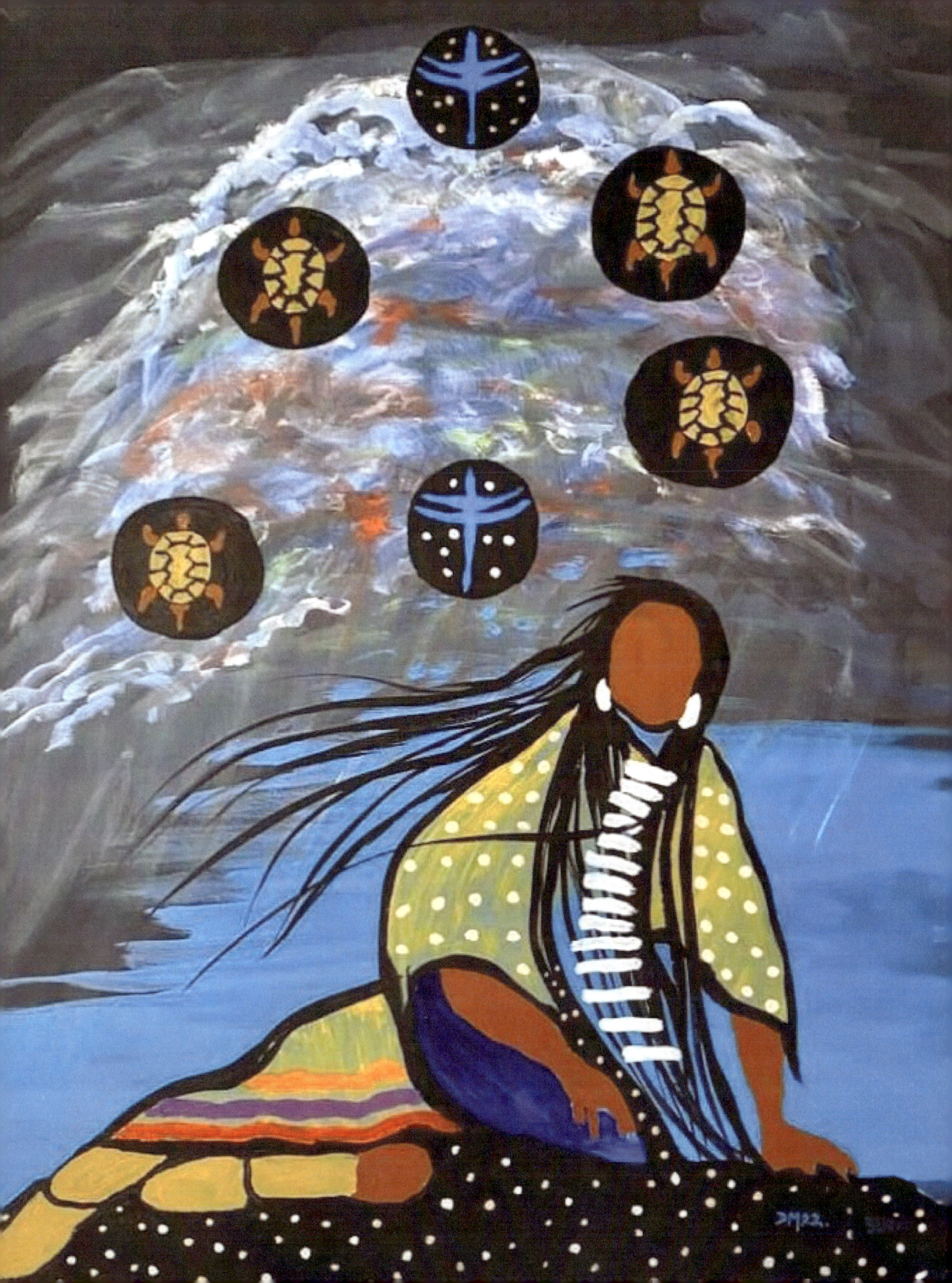

Unci—Grandmother

Her face is made from her Oyate (People), it is the cool breeze that rides with the stars. Unci thoughts are always strong, the beauty of a star and the bright sparkle you see once from her eyes always stay with you, and the guidance you feel makes your path. Her look is of warmth, these days when the heart makes you feel like a warm summer morning.

Unci is the stars that gather in a long path and wide during the night; this is her Oyate that comes and sees her; it is many.

Unci carries the tie that binds the circle; she sews together what we wear and also uses porcupine quills for our Oyate—pretty design patterns. I came to see Unci this morning, but Grandfather said she and other Winyans—Women had gone to pick timpsila—wild turnips along with two great warriors.

Tunkasila—Grandfather, let's make what horses need. I will wait for Unci. I will wait, but I hear her Ina—Mother calling, Toksa—until I see you again.

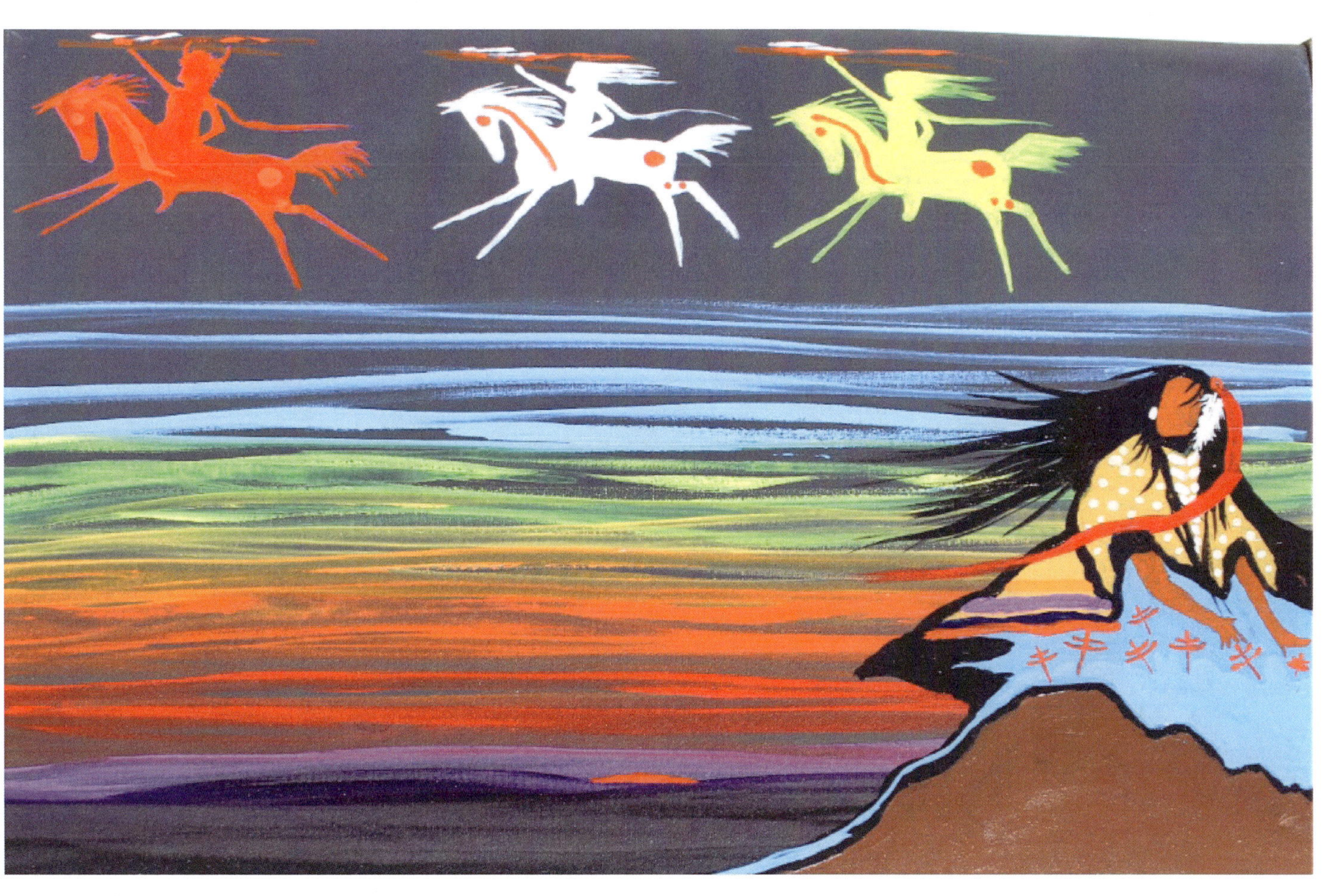

From Far Away

On a sunrise I came from Far away. I traveled with the wind from the north. I wondered how the strength of light could bring hope. If you see a light that looks like the sunrise, don't be afraid, it's just me, and the goodbyes don't come in my ride with this wind.

I only talk with the true light from my Soul, and my Mind, is already near your heart so from here until I see you again always know my light will guide your faith of Life.

Hecatu yelo—for I am prayer

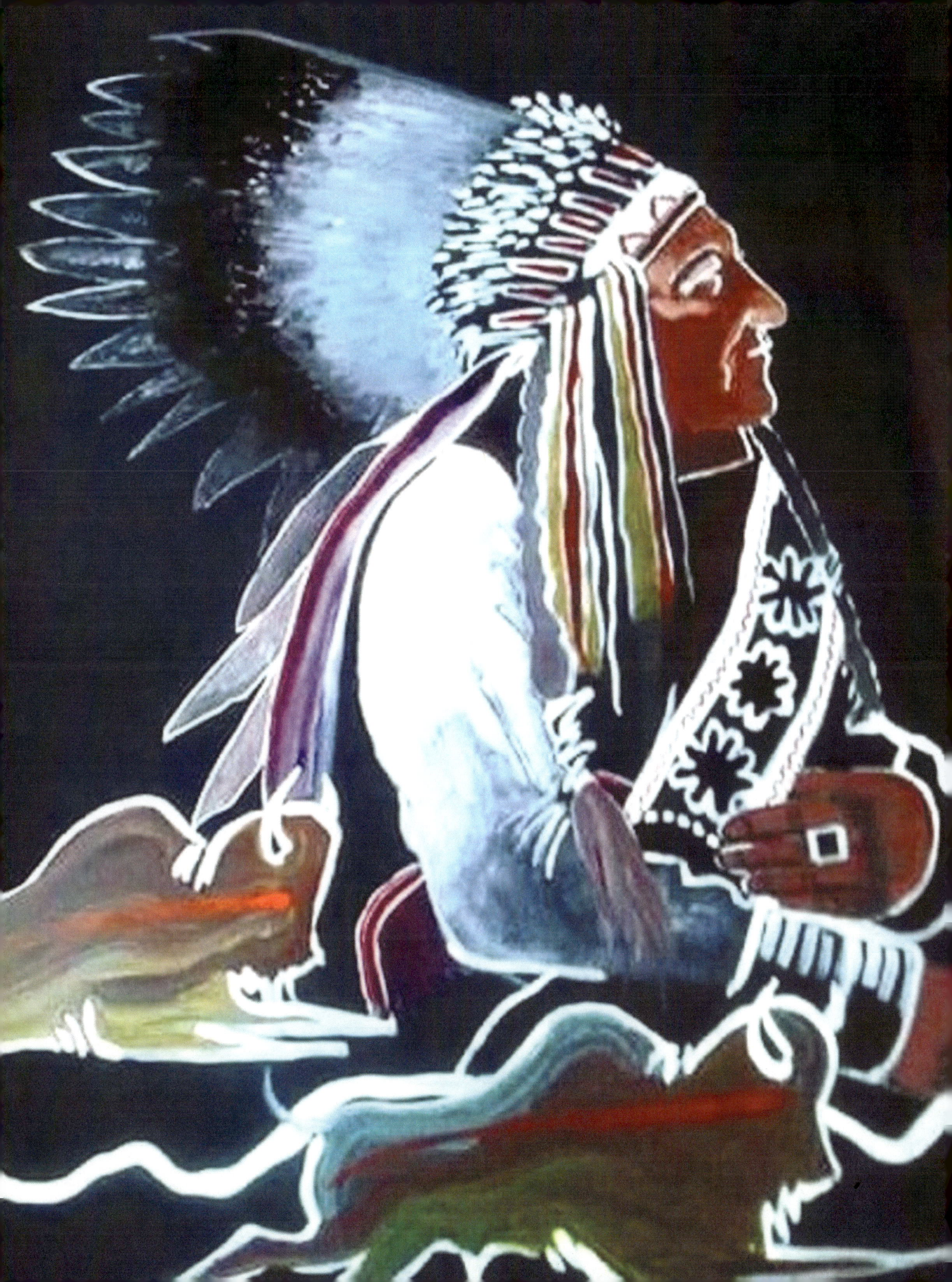

Star Children

She said, "Grandchildren, go into the universe I made. Your parent's have made stories and now live in the stars. Go by them, say hello, and go into the universe and live so your grandchildren can see and remember Unci (Grandmother) loves you.

They lived, and where they followed their parents and made a small little dipper and other stars and so now when the Earth's soul children go pray in their ceremonies and light using the fire, the smoke is a sign of saying thank you. It will rise into the universe. Go my grandchildren and shine.

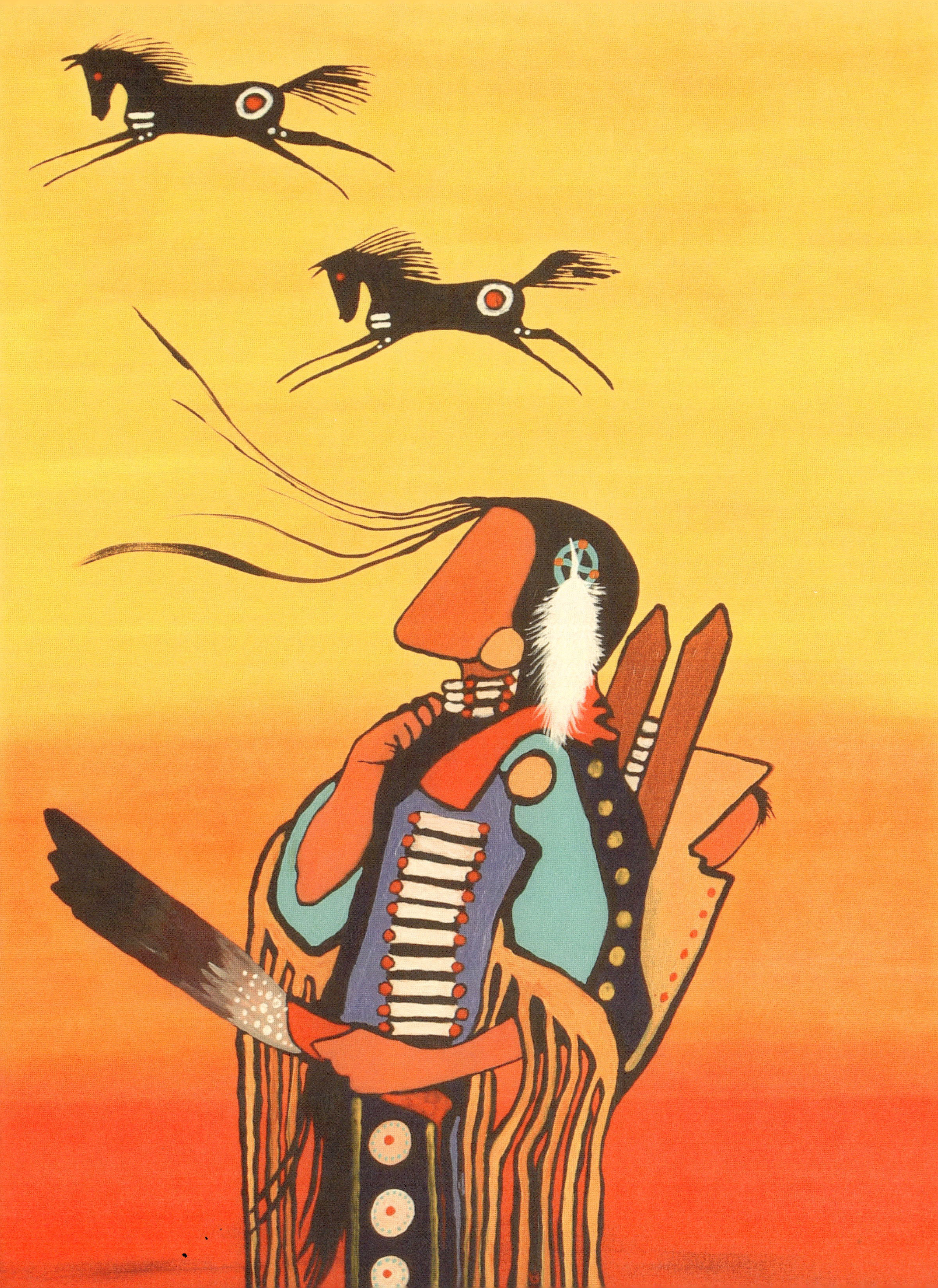

Keepers Of The Sky

They came to rest after a long journey to another place. They have been together forever. They left on a cold night to save others as the food and water was almost gone. They returned with blessings and the elements returned to keep their history alive. They were given honor so they were given immortality as heroes.

The gift given was to be the warriors whom will watch over their people and protect from above; the seven stars in the universe. So as We two legged came and fused our ways upon this land, we learned to have a precious friendship for We understand their healing and strength they give us, and so we look at it as big dipper keepers in the sky.

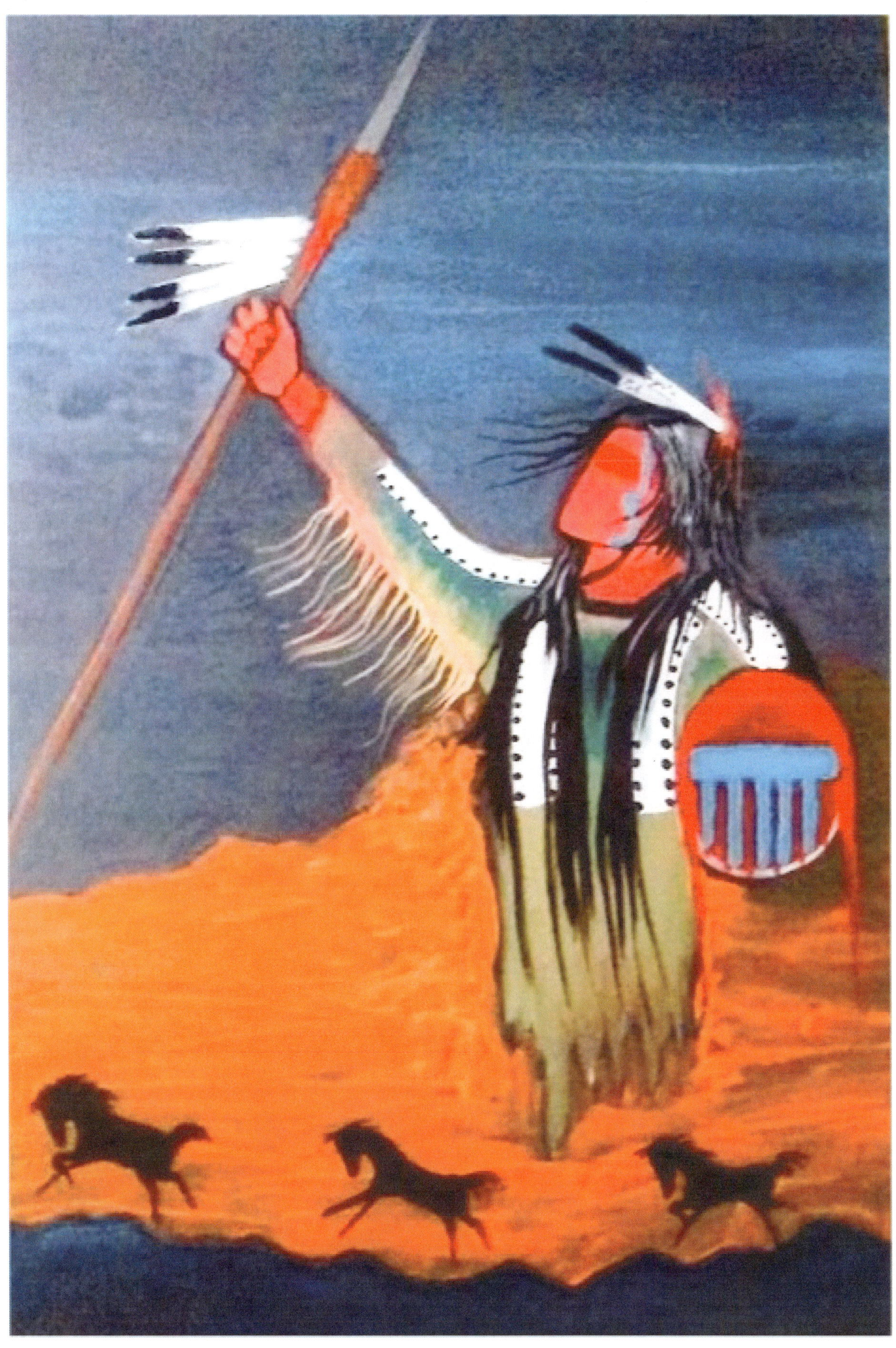

White Buffalo Calf Woman

The Unci (Grandmother) knew when she woke up that there was a ground that needed to be walked on. She had seen it in her dream. Then, she was driving and she saw the place of her dream and she stopped, got out, and walked over there. She closed her eyes and felt the breeze on her face and hair. She breathed in the fresh air and said, "I will be back. She went home instead of going where she was going, and she put on her regalia. The smell of fresh winter, soft leather put away. She prayed, she smudged herself, and regalia.

She took her eagle fan and sprinkled a little water on it as usual for the eagles thirst to be strong. She drove there and and played her song. It was herself. She was the beginning of the fresh spring weather coming back.

A meadowlark appeared and sang a beautiful song as she danced on the prairie. She smiled and knew the strength would be a Winyan of her people. All this time, she was a prayer for peace and blessings. The spirit had been in her life and now she knows for she is the White Buffalo Calf Woman.

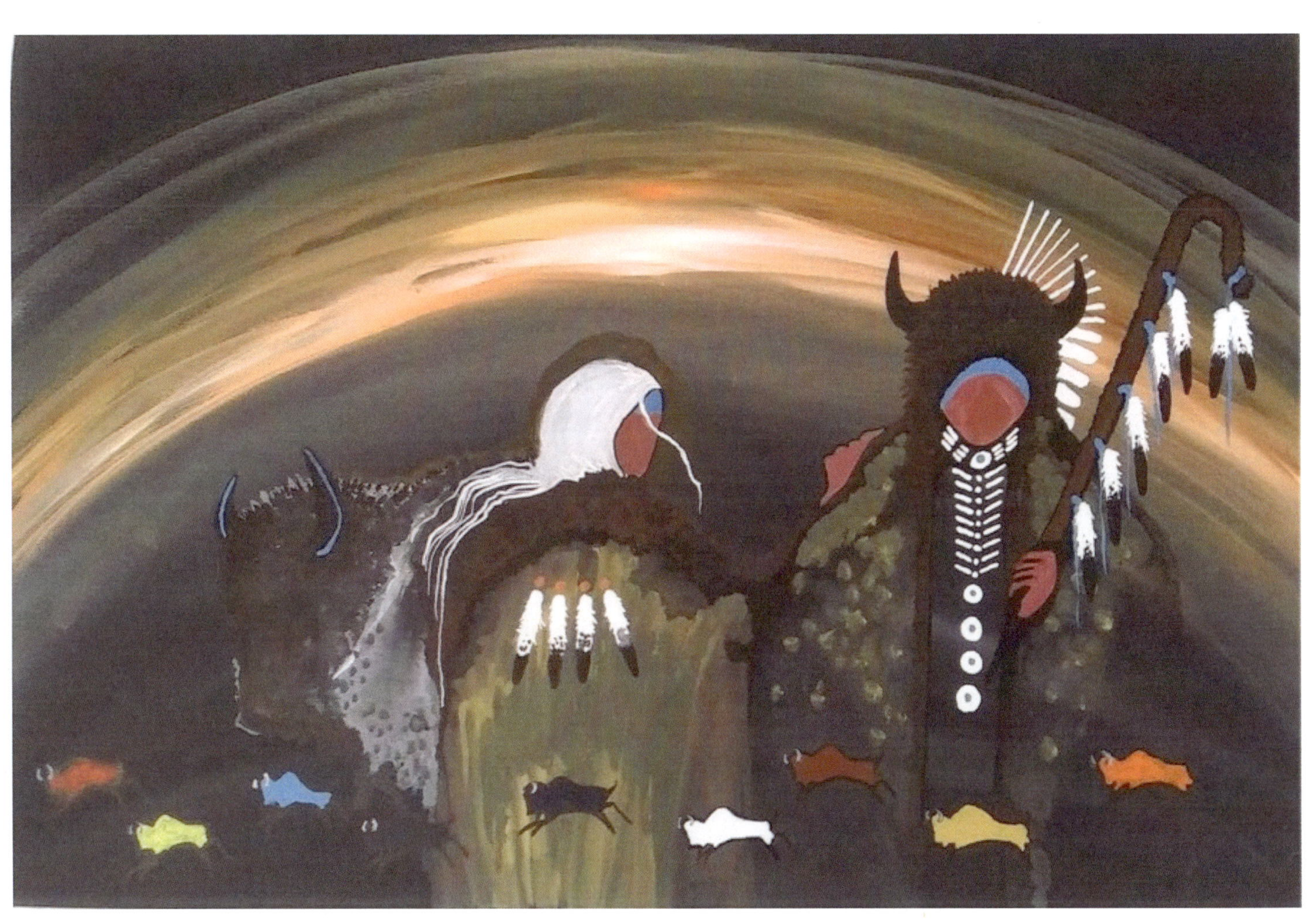

Nine Horse Bands

My People have the strongest and fastest of the paint horses. My uncles run the horses in the deep snow and make them run. They are trained for battle, ready for the Great Warriors. Their air is big so air breathing when running has different ways for a horse.

Grandfather said, horses are trained to run up hills. A slow walk to start, then when they are ready, they build up to a steady run. Then, when the air is strong in their insides and their back legs are strongest, they are pushed uphill alone. Then they are ready again. Riders are picked, for they are Great Warriors too. The horses together, they will protect our people from enemies.

Tasunke Witko (Crazy Horse)

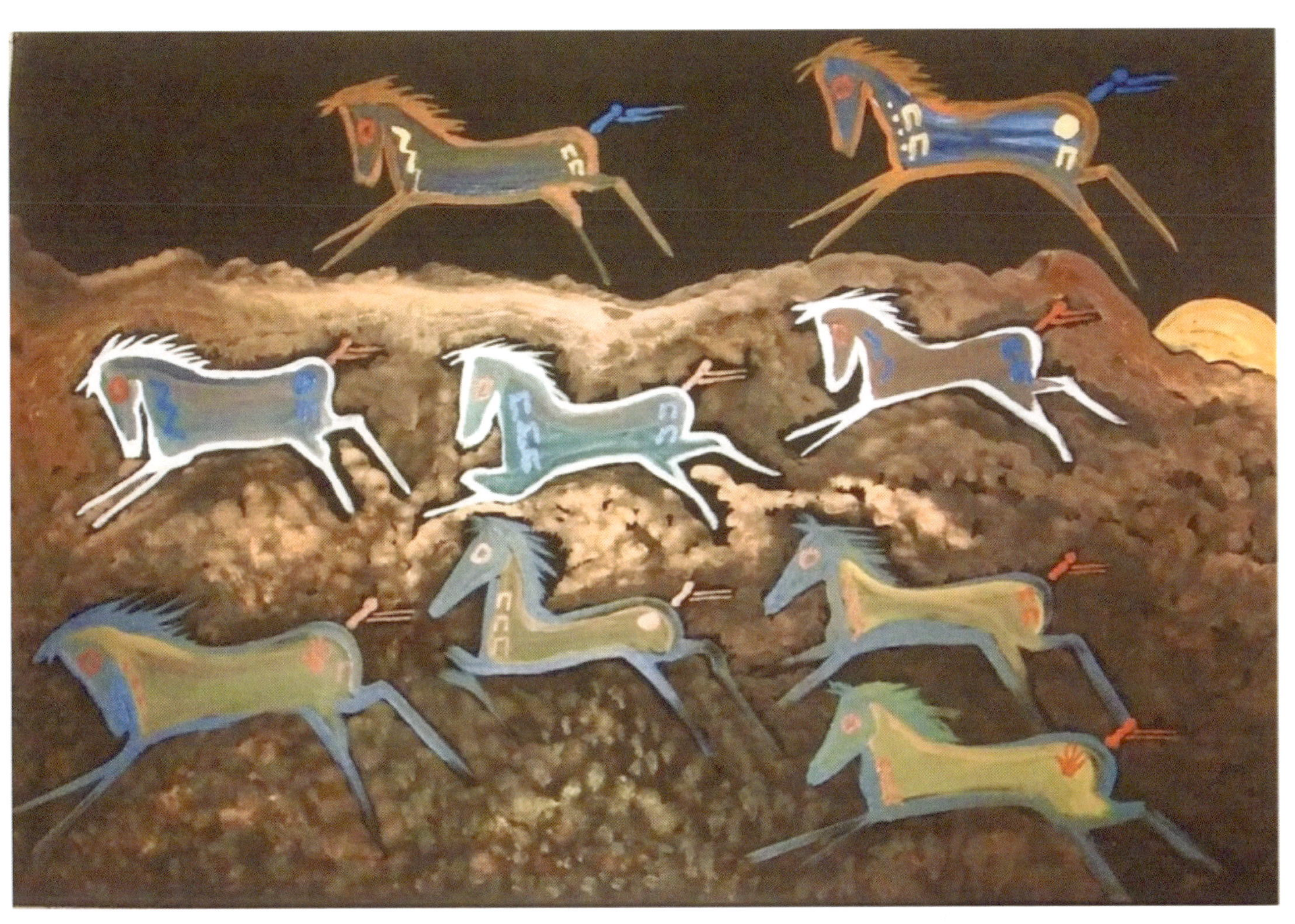

Sitting Bull

A horse came from somewhere. I don't know how it came in, but it stayed for two days. On the third morning, it went up on the hill looking north. Soon, the wind came, and the horse was still there. About noon, he came down to the river, walked through, and went back on the hill. That evening, the clouds started to gather into a thunderstorm with a lot of rain, and as it stood there, it looked like it had turned into a warrior. When lightning struck, the sky warrior was praying with a sacred cannupa, then the rain grew heavy, and the river became full.

The horses were now running with eagerness, and other animals were also. The lightning came and hit the ground near them, and a spirit appeared to put sage cedar sweetgrass and fresh grass down.

Morning came, and the horse was gone, but a white horse now lived among them. Years went by, and the horse traveled all over. One day, a man came, and the horse traveled with him. This man met a chief, and the man liked the chief, so he gave him the horse.

This is how Naca Sitting Bull got the beautiful white horse that could dance. Eventually, one morning, Sitting Bull died, and the horse started to dance, giving medicine to the Naca going on a journey.

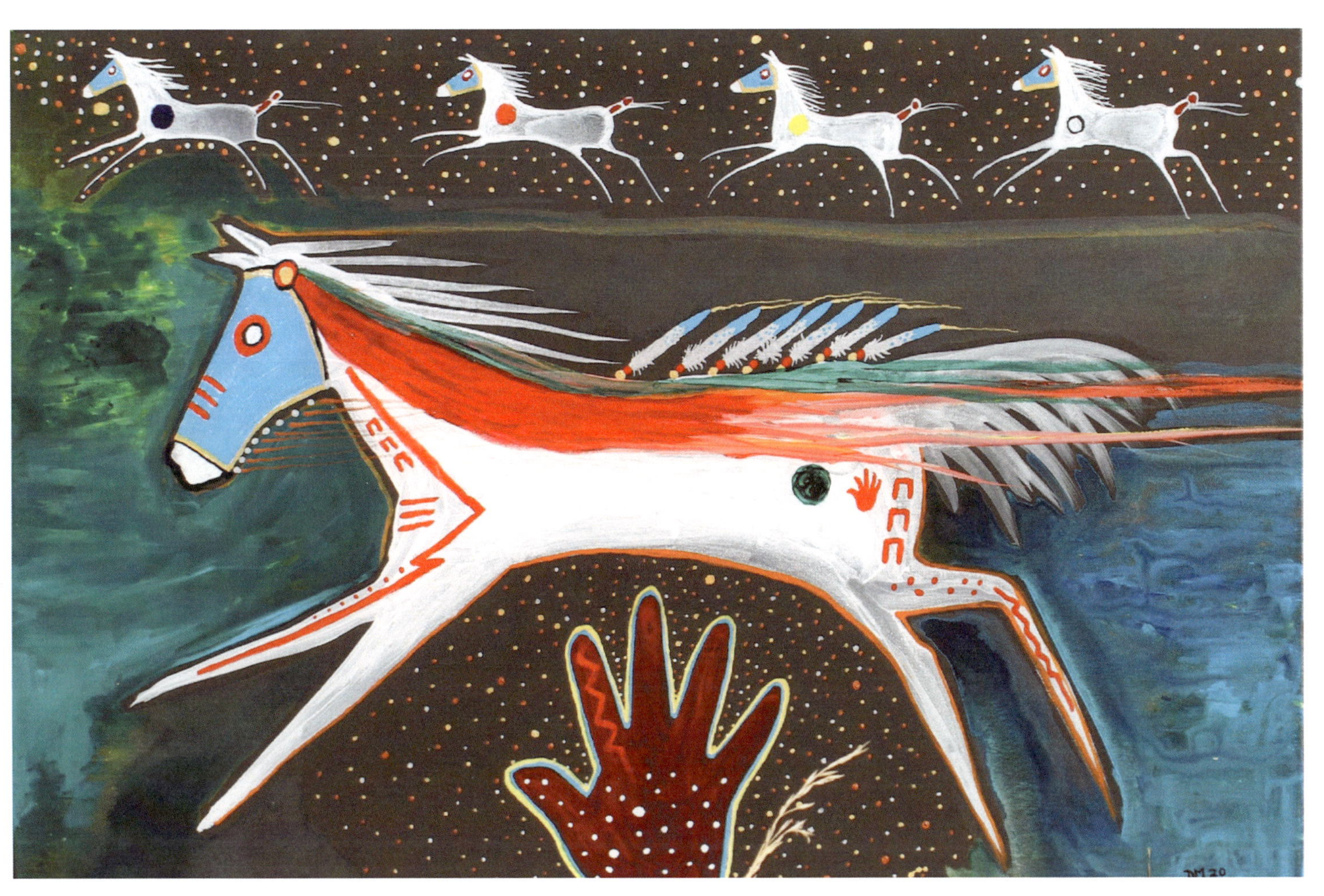

Happy Mother's Day

She gathered her belongings and made her way back to camp with her young daughter, who had a fondness for chokecherries. As they ascended a hill, she spotted the enemies of her tribe on the horizon. Stepping cautiously from tree to tree, she noticed a lone warrior on horseback, dressed in full war regalia. His long hair flowed in the breeze, his face painted boldly, projecting fearlessness.

Despite the danger, she maintained her composure, her courage fueled by the need to protect her child. The warrior noticed her; his gaze lingered, taking in the serene morning warmed by the sun. His majestic horse, also adorned with paint, shifted restlessly under him.

Sensing her predicament, the warrior guided his horse to block her from the view of the war party and gestured for her to quickly make her way through the ravine, which was covered with trees and bushes. Clutching her daughter, she hurried across the landscape. Glancing back, she met his eyes—one last look filled with tearful gratitude.

The warrior placed his hand over his heart and nodded solemnly before riding away. After a harrowing half-day's ride, she and her daughter reached the safety of their home. She recounted the encounter to her husband, who speculated about the mysterious warrior known to occasionally aid those in danger. "Perhaps he seeks peace among all," her husband mused, acknowledging the warrior's renowned fierceness among his own people.

That evening, as a gesture of thanks and protection, she burned sage, cedar, and sweetgrass. The family gathered in their tipi lodge, ending the day with nourishing food and heartfelt prayers, a quiet celebration of resilience and Mother's Day.

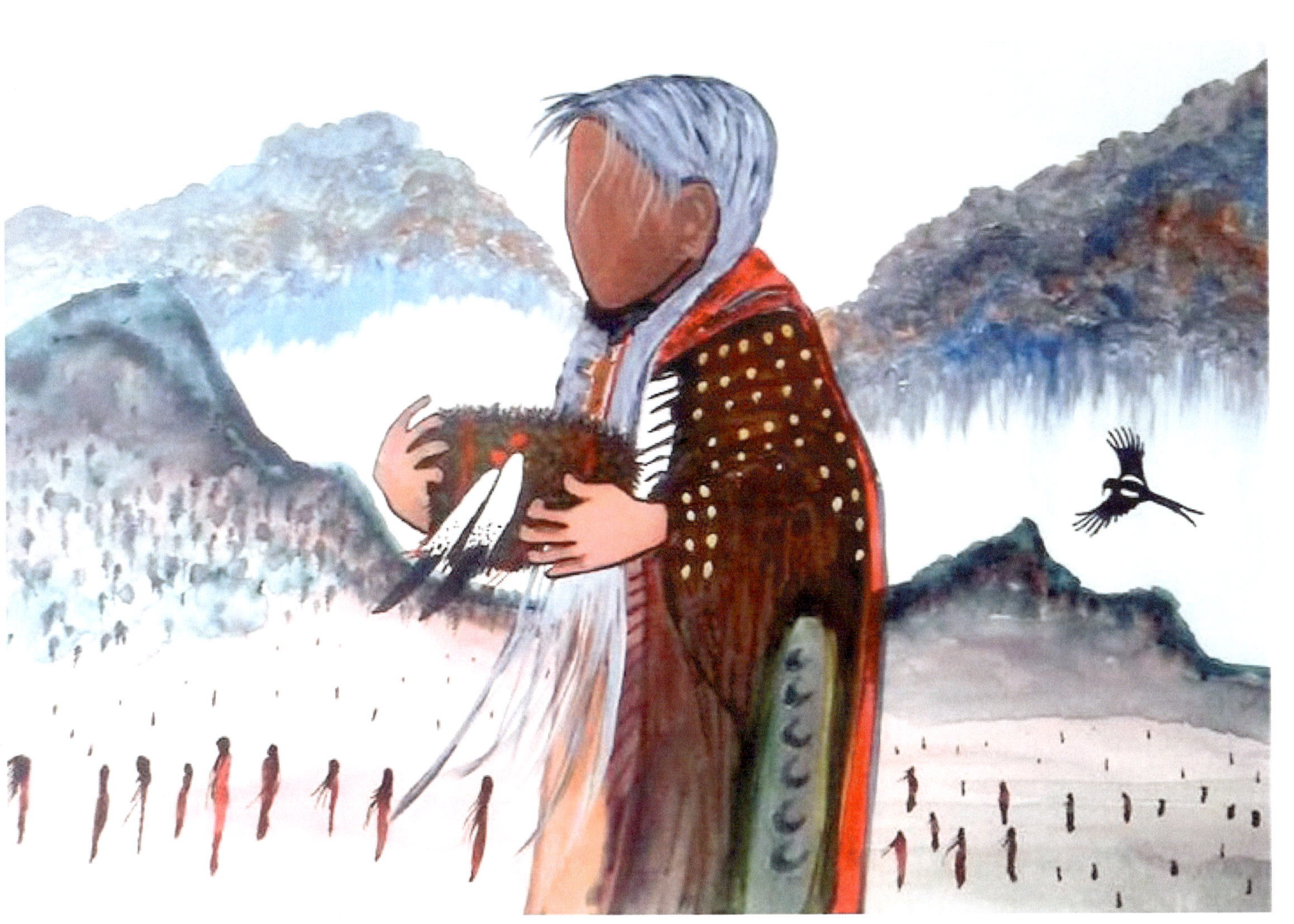

The Dreamer

He got off the bus 10 miles from the reservation, but he had no place to go and call home. Fresh from 4 years of service, he walked into an eating place with his duffle bag. The clean-cut look of a young marine fading into an old Soul from the fields of battle. He wanted to go back to the horses but didn't know if the horses he knew would still be there.

A long walk brought him to the reservation line and a car stopped. A woman driving the car asked if he wanted a ride. He got in and they talked until they got to the turn off towards the river road. The car left as he stood and looked at the old place of his days. An old friend was walking by, and he welcomed him back and invited him to stay a few days.

He grew a plan and borrowed tools to make his log cabin. He realized he had left his knife in the car of the woman as it had fallen out of his bag, so he cut with another knife. By the end of summer, he had a cabin, and it was home.

He went to the post office to organize for the military to send his checks. He asked bout that car, but no one knew.

After 5 years he was on his own work and a regular daily life. Then one day he rode upriver way out west on his horse. Old dusty roads covered with tall hard grass and rolling hills. On the horizon, he saw an old car much like the one he had seen long ago. He rode over there; his horse was jumpy and spooked but held strong. As he looked on the floor he saw his old knife. The plates said 1968. No tires, just rims. He looked and he knew this place. In his heart he knew he was here before. In a ceremony later, he was told after what he said in a prayer that the water keeper said welcome home. You've been here all the time. He was the Dreamer. The Holy Man. Hecatu yelo—prayers.

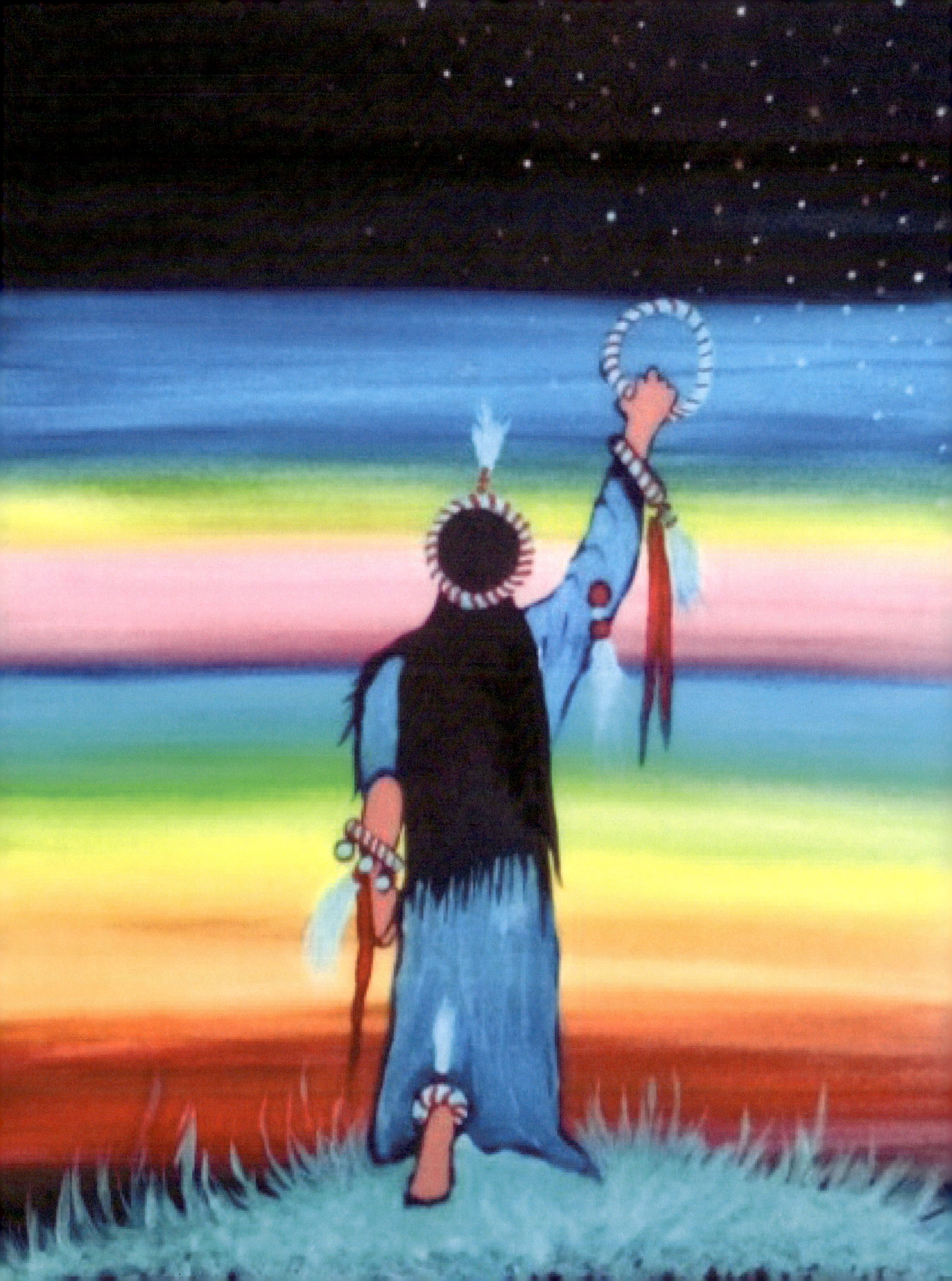

The Old Newspaper

Uncle discovered an old newspaper in the glove compartment of a vintage car. The newspaper featured a circled advertisement showcasing plates and silverware alongside a captivating image of a red-tail hawk. Curious, he noted an address listed on the ad and looked it up, finding that it originated from California. Eager to learn more, he showed the newspaper to his wife who encouraged him to investigate further.

Following her advice, Uncle drove to the post office to inquire if the store mentioned in the advertisement was still in operation. Upon confirmation, he placed an order for the items to be delivered. Three years later, a delivery truck pulling a trailer arrived at his house. The driver approached Uncle, verifying the address and asking if he was the intended recipient. He explained that the kitchenware was a belated birthday gift for a widow whose husband, a World War II veteran, had never returned home. He had intended it as a birthday present for her.

Just then, a red-tail hawk soared overhead. Uncle mused aloud about finding the hawk's image in that old newspaper, suggesting a serendipitous connection. The delivery driver smiled, remarking that perhaps Uncle had metaphorically brought the veteran home with this thoughtful gift. With a sense of closure and goodwill, the driver left, leaving behind not just the kitchenware but a story of remembrance and a red feather as a symbol of this poignant reunion.

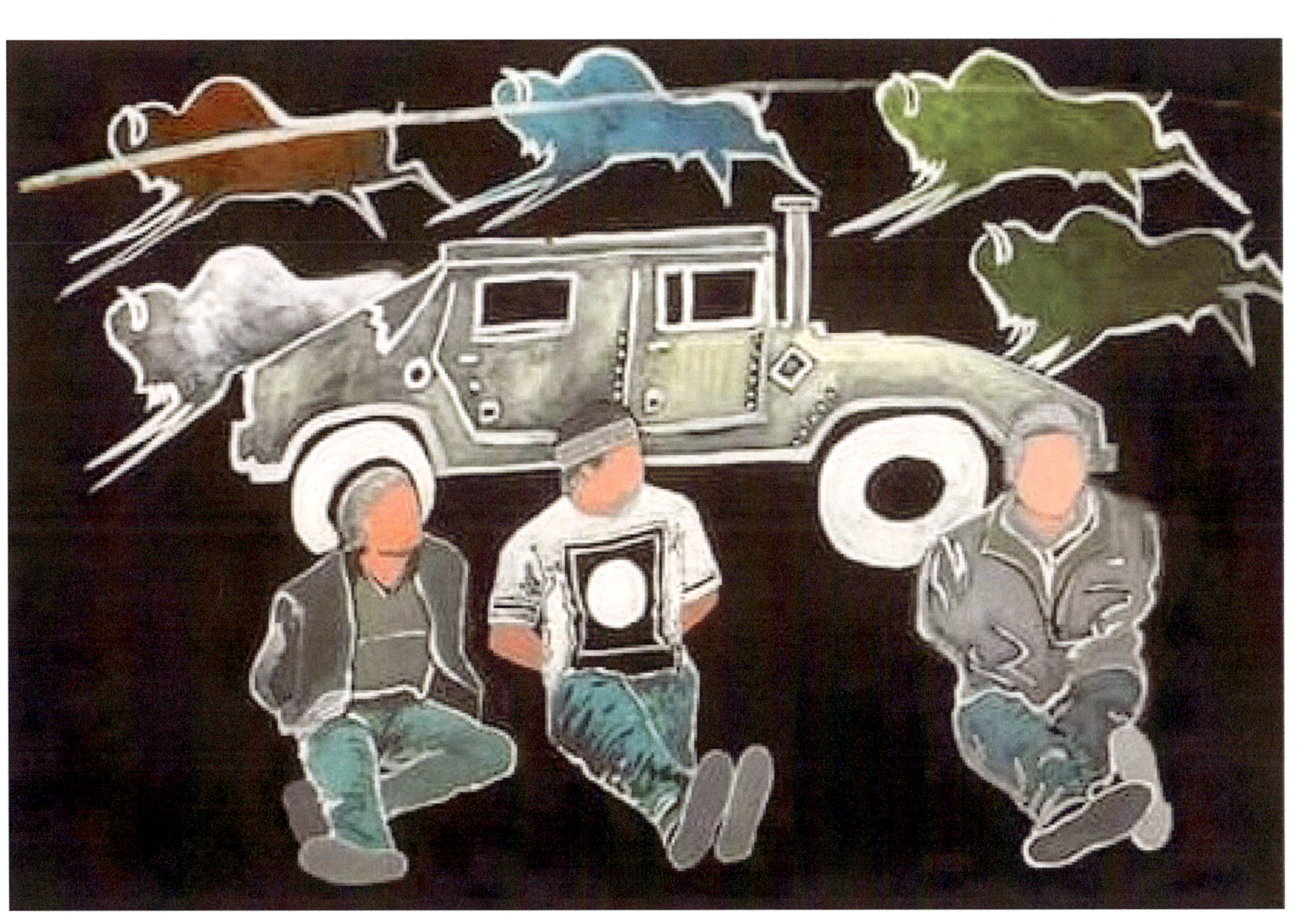

Tom Mix The Rooster

Tom Mix, the rooster, was notorious for causing chaos at the ranch. One evening, his antics led to disaster when he knocked over a kerosene lamp hanging from a pole. The fire blazed brightly, causing the horses to run wild and Scooter, the ranch dog, to dart off in panic.

Hector, a Mexican ranch hand, rushed out to tackle the flames. He grabbed a bucket of water and attempted to douse the fire, muttering in Spanish as he worked. Overhearing Hector, the ranch's parrot joined in the commotion, repeatedly squawking "Get the tequila! Get the tequila!" in a comic mimicry.

In the midst of this chaos, Fettus, a small mule known for his stubbornness, trotted over and seemed to throw in his two cents about the situation. The noise and confusion roused the ranch owner, who poked his head out the window. Spotting the flickering firelight and the scattered animals, he mistakenly yelled to his wife, Mabel, "Wake up! Indians outside—a war party!"

Mabel, unimpressed and aware of the true year being 2021, dryly replied, "What the heck, go back to bed."

Eventually, the fire was extinguished, and calm returned. But Tom Mix continued his raucous crowing, urging everyone to "Get up, get up!" as if still in the midst of the emergency. By evening, the only bird making any noise was the parrot, who had amusingly relocated the lamp to the very pole Tom Mix favored each morning.

With the lamp in its new place and the memory of the evening's events still fresh, Fettus quietly assumed the role of the new character to watch in the unfolding drama of the ranch.

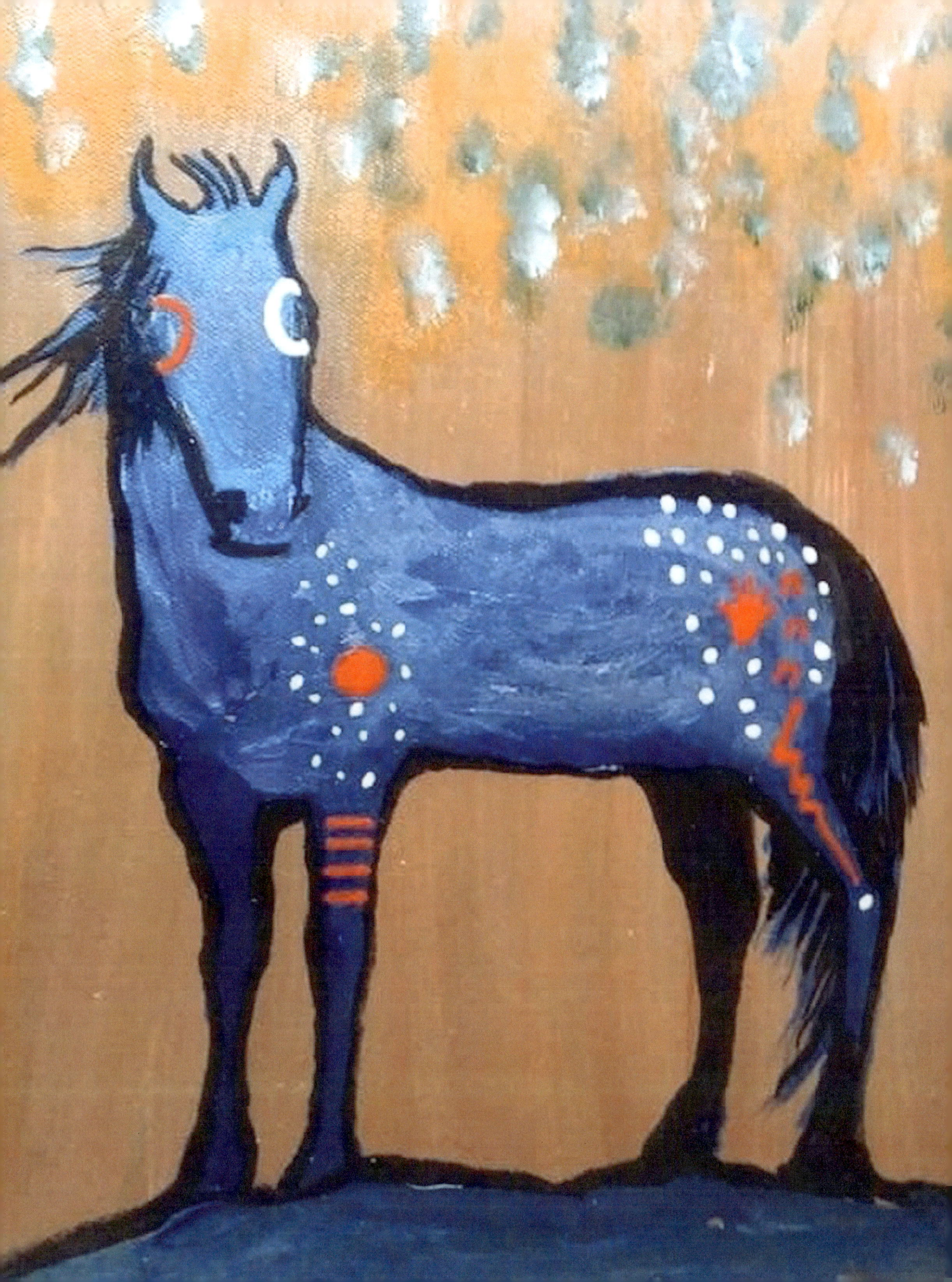

Young Poke

Young Poke arrived at the ranch riding an ATV, stirring up dust as he went. Old Timer (OT), overseeing the morning's work, greeted him casually. "You're the new hire, huh?" Young Poke confirmed with a nonchalant "yup." OT, laying out the day's plan, suggested, "I'll head north, you take the east. We'll locate the grazers and then strategize on driving them back to the ranch."

With a smirk, Young Poke quipped, "Hope your horse can keep up." OT simply tipped his hat and rode off. By afternoon, OT had successfully herded about 23 grazers towards the valley, careful to keep the newborns close to the ranch. Meanwhile, he noticed a disturbance; the grazers were scattering, driven by the noisy ATV.

When the engine fell silent, OT approached to find Young Poke dismounted, the ATV out of gas. "I ran out," Poke admitted sheepishly. OT nodded, "Stay put. I'll round up the rest." Skillfully, OT gathered the scattered grazers with the help of others, securing them in the pasture before closing the gate.

Back at the ranch, OT realized they were out of gas, with the owners away in town. Resourceful, he fetched John Wayne, a sturdy Shetland pony, and delivered it to Young Poke as the sun set. With no other options, Young Poke rode the pony back to the ranch.

The day's events offered Young Poke valuable lessons: always prepare and check your resources, and sometimes, traditional methods—like walking with the grazers—earn you more respect than modern conveniences.

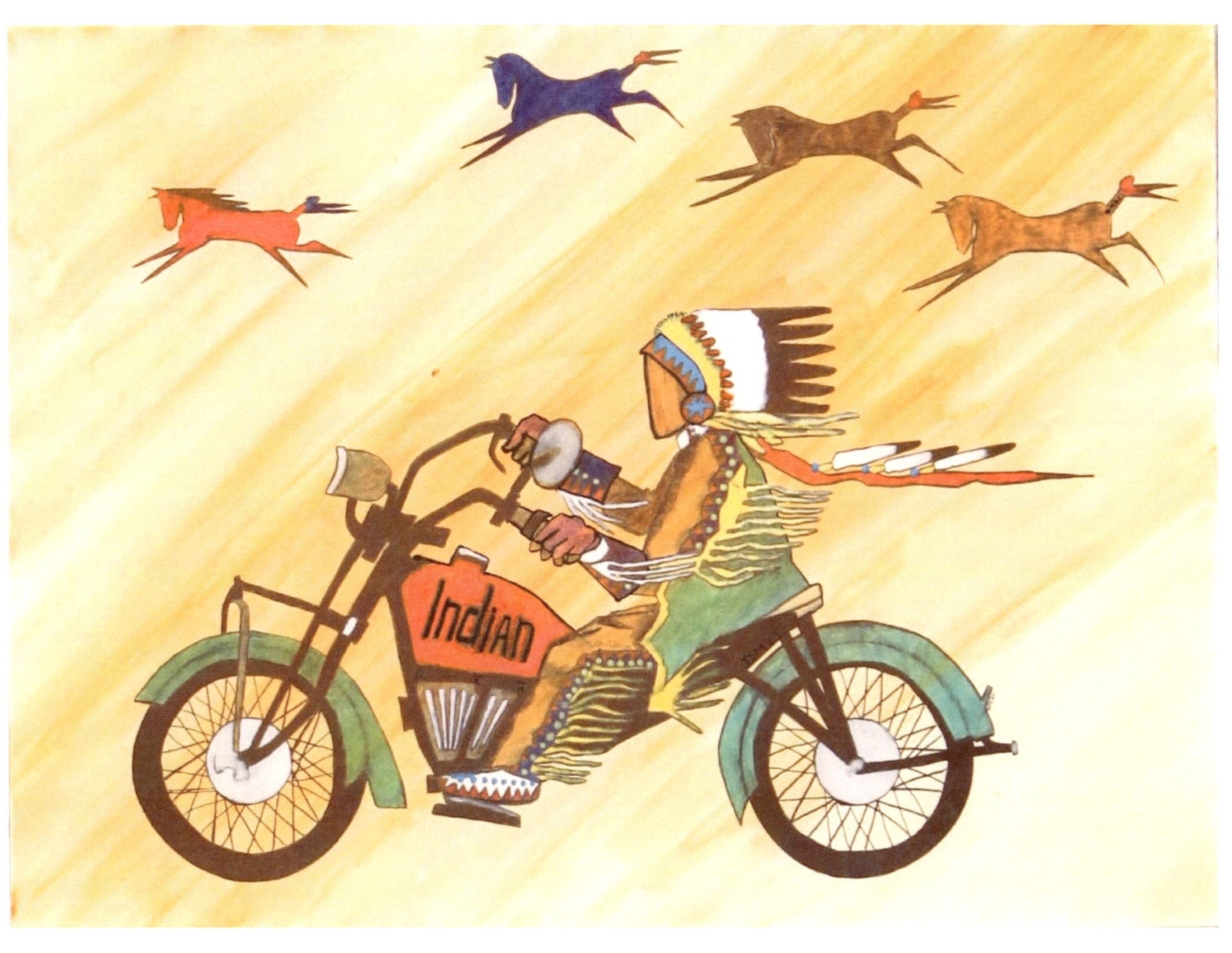
Indian

The Warrior

A warrior set out to hunt game to sustain his tribe through the fall. As he approached the great river, he paused to check his supplies, draw water from the clear stream, and attend to his horse. Suddenly, the horse's ears perked up and shifted sideways, alerting the warrior to nearby movement. Calming the horse, the warrior looked downstream and noticed a figure approaching—a woman supporting a wounded warrior, his condition evident from the blood staining his clothes.

As the pair drew closer, the warrior instinctively gripped his knife, ready for any threat. However, he was struck by the sight of the woman, her long black hair matted by tears, clearly distraught from long hours of crying. They stopped near him, and he hurried to assist, laying his buffalo robe by the shore to rest the injured man.

The woman communicated through sign language that the warrior was dying. Despite the grave wounds, the hunter did his best to help. As the wounded man passed away in her arms, the woman's grief deepened into the evening. She attempted to offer the hunter a gift in gratitude, which he initially declined but eventually accepted.

Before the woman's arrival, the hunter had heard a mysterious, beautiful sound, which vanished as they appeared. Now, as he prepared to wrap the deceased in the buffalo robe, he realized the woman's gift was a leather bag containing a stick with holes—it was a flute.

As the evening turned to night, the woman transformed into a woodpecker and flew away, leaving the warrior alone. He returned to his tribe with the game and, exhausted, retreated to a hill to rest. As the wind blew through the flute, it recreated the enchanting sounds he had heard by the river, captivating him and his people alike.

In time, he mastered the flute, enchanting the valley with melodies that stirred romantic feelings among the young men and women of his tribe. As an old warrior, he continued to play until the end of his days, when the woodpecker returned to sing for him one last time. Through his journey, he introduced the haunting beauty of flute music to the Lakota people, leaving a lasting legacy.

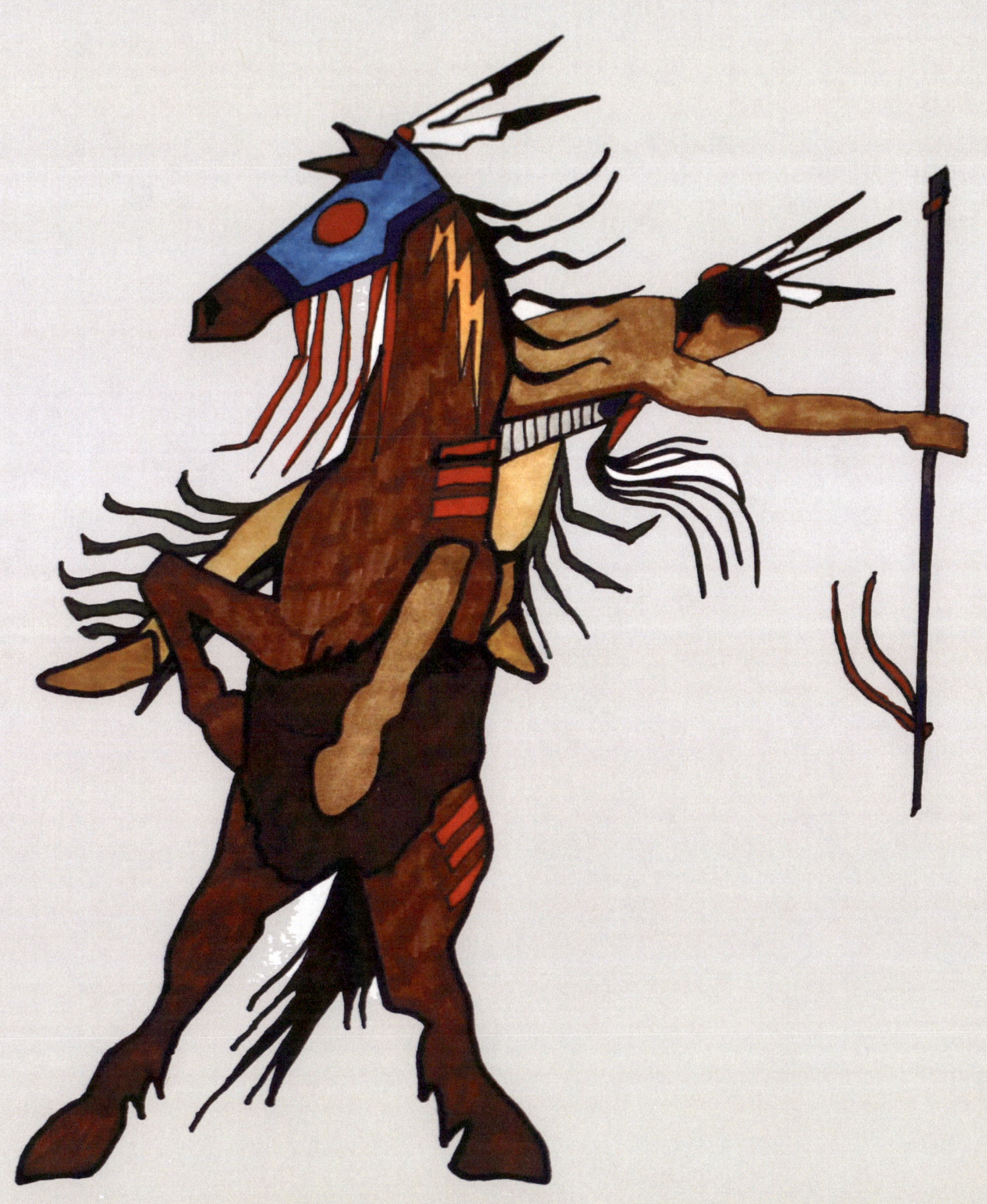

About The Author and Artist

Darrell Marcus Kills In Sight - Wambli Ohitika (Brave Eagle)

Darrell is a last-generation fluent Lakota speaker from Spring Creek, Rosebud Sioux—Sicangu tribe, Rosebud Reservation, South Dakota. A direct family descendant of the Crazy Horse family.—Ta'sunka Witko Tiospaye. His generational family stories of Lakota traditional culture are written through prose with an antidotal message of hope, healing, and preservation.

Lakota traditional cultural and spiritual values reflect the natural world, the importance of family, and having courage, strength, and survival for the generations to come. A message for all ages in a modern time.

"My legacy of reflection is my life's journey. Language is important. When it is gone, then the artworks and words of life are only memorized by you. I am the grandson of Naca—Chiefs & Warriors—and Crazy Horse. It's all I have needed to live this Far. Hecatu yelo—in good prayers." DM

Original paintings by Lakota artist Darrell Marcus Kills In Sight. Acrylic on canvas.

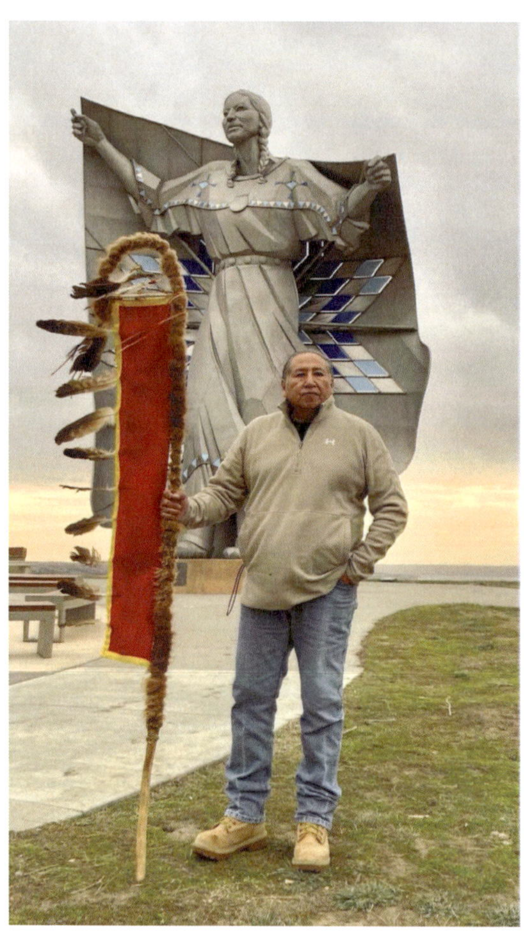

Darrell Marcus—Homeland: Rosebud, South Dak'ota

www.ingramcontent.com/pod-product-compliance
Lightning Source LLC
LaVergne TN
LVRC090254110826
845147LV00008B/737

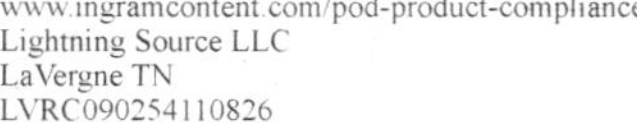

* 9 7 9 8 9 9 0 5 2 1 7 1 1 *